D0032996

POWERPUFF PROFESSOR

by Amy Keating Rogers

SCHOLASTIC INC.

New York   Toronto   London   Auckland   Sydney
Mexico City   New Delhi   Hong Kong

If you purchased this book without a cover, you should be aware that this book is stolen property. It was reported as "unsold and destroyed" to the publisher, and neither the author nor the publisher has received any payment for this "stripped book."

No part of this publication may be reproduced in whole or in part, or stored in a retrieval system, or transmitted in any form or by any means, electronic, mechanical, photocopying, recording, or otherwise, without written permission of the publisher. For information regarding permission, write to Scholastic Inc., Attention: Permissions Department, 555 Broadway, New York, NY 10012.

ISBN 0-439-16019-7

Copyright © 2000 by Cartoon Network.
THE POWERPUFF GIRLS and all related characters and elements are trademarks of Cartoon Network © 2000.
CARTOON NETWORK and logo are trademarks of Cartoon Network © 2000.
Published by Scholastic Inc. All rights reserved.
SCHOLASTIC and associated logos are trademarks and/or registered trademarks of Scholastic Inc.

Designed by Peter Koblish

12 11 10 9 8 7   0 1 2 3 4 5/0

Printed in the U.S.A.
First Scholastic printing, March 2000

SUGAR . . .

SPICE . . .

AND EVERYTHING NICE . . .

These were the ingredients chosen to

create the perfect little girls.

But Professor Utonium accidentally

added an extra ingredient to

the concoction —

CHEMICAL X!

And thus, the Powerpuff Girls were born!

Using their ultra superpowers,

BLOSSOM,

BUBBLES,

and **BUTTERCUP**

have dedicated their lives to fighting crime

and the forces of evil!

Chapter 1

The city of Townsville! Where another wonderful weekend was beginning on a beautiful Saturday morning.

Blossom, Buttercup, and Bubbles were very excited. They were going to spend some family time with the Professor this weekend!

"This is going to be the best!" Buttercup said happily. Her dark eyes flashed with excitement.

"Yeah, we've been so busy fighting crime," Blossom agreed. "It seems like

1

forever since we got to hang out with the Professor."

"I'll bet he has some super plans for us!" Bubbles said.

"Girls! Breakfast is served!" the Professor called.

In a flash, the Girls were down the stairs and at the table.

"What's for breakfast, Professor?" Bubbles asked, taking her seat.

"I'm starving!" Buttercup announced. "Fill me up! I hope it's waffles and bacon and pancakes and sausage and eggs — my favorite!" she exclaimed.

The Professor smiled with pride. He had the most wonderful little girls anyone could wish for. He set their meals before them.

The three Girls' eyes grew wide. The Professor had prepared a perfect meal for each one of them.

In front of Bubbles sat a pale blue plate stacked with pancakes. They had great big smiley faces on them.

"Oh, Professor," Bubbles said with glee, "these are the sweetest pancakes ever. They're almost too cute to eat!"

"Well, you go ahead and eat those pancakes, Bubbles," the Professor replied. "Then the happy pancakes will be inside you for a happy day!"

Buttercup's green plate was piled high with sausage and bacon and eggs. There was even a little waffle on the side, just the way Buttercup liked it.

3

"Yum!" Buttercup said. She looked at the huge meal in awe. "This is a meal fit for . . . "

"A superstrong fighter?" the Professor asked.

"Yeah!" Buttercup replied, digging into her sausage. The Professor knew that she liked a strength-building meal so she could be a superstrong superhero.

But Blossom was confused by the meal on her pink plate. There was a piece of fish, some broccoli, and blueberries. If Bubbles's smiling pancakes were supposed to give her a happy day, and Buttercup's breakfast was supposed to make her a tough fighter, what was her meal for?

"Professor, what kind of breakfast is this?" Blossom asked.

"Why, Blossom, that's brain food," the Professor replied. "Starting the day with these vitamin-rich foods will build your brainpower!"

Blossom smiled.

The Girls dove into their food. It was truly delicious. Even Blossom's!

"Well, Girls, I have a special day planned for the four of us," the Professor told them.

The Girls began to bounce up and down in their seats.

"What is it?" Blossom asked. "What's the plan?"

The Professor smiled. "I've packed the car with our blankets, towels, and toys. So as soon as you're done eating, we'll head to — the beach!"

"Yay!" the Girls shouted. They hadn't been to the beach in such a long time. They always seemed to be busy beating up monsters and fighting crime. But today was going to be different.

Then just as they were changing into their bathing suits, their special hot line telephone began to ring.

Hurry, Girls! It's the hot line!

Chapter 2

Beep! Beep! Beep!

Blossom answered the phone. "Powerpuff hot line!"

"Hello, Blossom," the voice on the other end said. "This is the Mayor." The Mayor called the Girls on the hot line whenever Townsville was in trouble and needed their help.

"Hello, Mayor. What's the trouble?" Blossom asked.

Bubbles and Buttercup hovered anxiously nearby.

"There's a terrible monster destroying Townsville," the Mayor told Blossom. "We need you right away."

"We'll be right there, Mayor!" Blossom promised. "Come on, Girls, Townsville needs us."

"We're right behind you," Buttercup said. "Oh, but what about the beach?"

"Yeah, and the Professor!" Bubbles added.

"Okay, let's fight the monster really quickly," Blossom said. "Then we can still make it to the beach."

The Girls went downstairs. They found the Professor dressed in his plaid swim trunks. He had special shades clipped to his square, black-rimmed glasses. His nose was smeared with thick white sunscreen.

"Are you ready to go, Girls?" he asked.

"Sorry, Professor, but the Mayor called," Blossom told him. "We have to go fight a monster."

"But we'll fight him superquick," Buttercup said.

"And we'll hurry right back," Bubbles promised.

"That's okay, Girls. You go do your duty," the Professor said. "The city needs your help."

The Girls headed off to save the day. The Professor waved as they left. Then he sat down on the couch with a thump.

The Girls will be back soon, he thought.

So he waited.

And waited.

And waited . . .

Late that night, the Powerpuff Girls finally arrived back home. It had taken a lot longer to fight the monster than they had expected. The monster had sharp black spikes on its skin that it shot like spears. In the end, the Girls had combined their powers to send out a special triple-thick supershield. The spikes had bounced off the shield and back at the monster. The Powerpuff Girls had saved Townsville as usual, but it had been an all-day battle.

The Girls flew slowly into the house. They were so pooped they could barely hover above the ground. On their way to bed, they passed by the dining room and saw the Professor asleep at his place at the table. The big dinner plate in front of him was empty. But the plates for the Girls were heaped with food.

The Professor woke up with a start. "Girls! You're home!" he cried happily.

"Yeah. Sorry we're so late, Professor," Blossom said. "The monster was much tougher to fight than we thought."

"Aw, he wasn't that tough," Buttercup said, yawning and rubbing her eyes.

"Anyway, we're sorry," Bubbles said.

"We'll make it up to you tomorrow," Buttercup promised.

"Well, at least sit down and have the nice meal I cooked before you head off to bed," the Professor said. "That way we can talk about your day."

"Oh, thanks, Professor, but we're much too tired to eat," Blossom said. She was barely able to hold her head up.

The three Girls collapsed on the floor, asleep.

The Professor shook his head. He picked up the three Girls, carried them upstairs, and tucked them in.

Poor sleepy Girls, he thought. Well, tomorrow we'll have a great day.

chapter 4

The next morning!

When the Girls woke up after a long night's sleep, the Professor was waiting for them. He was grinning from ear to ear.

"I have a great plan for today," he announced. "We're going to see *The TV Puppet Pals Movie.*"

"Yay!" the Girls shouted.

The TV Puppet Pals was the Girls' favorite show. They watched it every night before they went to bed. Mitch and Clem were the two puppets. They told jokes and said funny things.

"I love Mitch and Clem," Bubbles said happily.

"TV Puppet Pals are the greatest!" Buttercup agreed.

"And the movie is supposed to be super," Blossom added.

"Well, let's hurry," the Professor said. "We don't want to miss it!"

The four of them hurried off. At the theater, the Professor bought each Girl her own popcorn and soda.

"Can I have mine with extra butter?" Bubbles asked.

"You bet!" The Professor smiled. "Anything for my Girls!"

The lights dimmed, and the movie began. Everybody was happy. Finally, they

were having a fun family day.

But suddenly, just a few minutes into the movie . . .

Crash! Boom! Bam!

A big, green, slimy monster tore through the movie screen. The crowd began to scream and run.

"Powerpuff Girls! Help!" a man screamed.

The Girls looked up. The monster was towering above them, holding a bunch of people in his hand. Green slime dripped all over.

"Come on, Girls!" Blossom shouted. "The monster's attacking."

"Let's get 'em!" Buttercup yelled.

Bubbles sighed. "Why couldn't the monster have waited until after the movie?"

The Girls flew into action. But the monster had already begun to stomp down the street.

"Sorry, Professor!" the Girls called as they flew after the monster.

"Oh, that's okay, Girls," the Professor said with a smile. "I understand. You go stop that monster."

But as soon as the Girls were gone, the Professor's smile faded away. He walked sadly up the aisle of the theater. The four of them had been having such a good time.

But now it was just an-
other day alone.

The Professor drove
home to do some work.
In his lab, he gazed at a
framed picture of him-
self with the Girls. They
were all smiling and
having a great time.

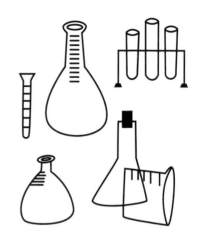

If only there was a way to
spend more time with the Girls. He didn't
care where or how.

That gave the Professor an idea.

"That's it!" he shouted. He put down
the picture and ran into his lab, slamming
the door after him. From behind the
door, there were sounds of sawing,
drilling, and hammering.

Go, Professor! Go!

Chapter 5

Meanwhile, in downtown Townsville, the Girls were busy fighting the green slime monster.

Buttercup flew in and gave him a superkick to the belly. But the monster shot green slime out of his stomach, knocking her down.

Bubbles socked him in the nose. He swatted at her with his sticky hand, sending her flying.

Finally, Blossom shot at him with her eye beams. But the monster sent out a slippery green shield to protect himself. Blossom's beams bounced off it and came back at her.

The monster began to crush cars and tear up buildings. But the Powerpuff Girls were not ready to give up. They'd been in tougher fights than this.

"Plug him up, Girls!" Blossom shouted.

Buttercup and Bubbles flew straight into the monster's nostrils. He couldn't breathe. His nose tickled. His eyes began to water. Blossom flew around and grabbed him by the tail. Suddenly, the monster sneezed. Bubbles and Buttercup shot out of his nostrils, all covered with green monster nose-goo. The monster flung Blossom with his tail.

All three Girls sailed through the air and crashed into a building.

The monster stomped through the city. He ripped up the Townsville Museum and tossed it in the air. Then he smashed the Townsville Bridge. Cars toppled off into the water. Next he set the Townsville Forest on fire with his monster breath. Finally, he caught a plane in the sky and threw it toward Townsville Volcano Mountain.

The Girls zipped back into action. Bubbles soared to the museum and snatched it before it smashed to the ground. Buttercup pulled the bridge back together and rescued all the cars. Blossom extinguished the forest fire with her super ice breath.

But the plane was still heading toward the mountain. It was about to crash!

Out of nowhere, a white streak crossed the sky.

"What's that?" Blossom asked.

"A bird?" Bubbles guessed.

"A plane?" Buttercup suggested.

The white streak raced toward the plane. It swooped just in time to save the plane!

The Girls were amazed. They were even more amazed to discover the mysterious hero was none other than . . .

. . . the Professor!

He was all dressed up in a white jumpsuit with a silver lab coat and a little silver cape. On his feet were silver boots; on his head, a white helmet. In place of his usual square, black-rimmed glasses were silver goggles.

"Never fear! The Powerpuff Professor is here!" he shouted.

"Professor!" the Girls shouted.

"You can fly!" Buttercup cried.

"You have superstrength!" Blossom added.

"And you look so cute in that suit!" Bubbles commented.

"No time to explain, Girls. I've got a monster to fight!" the Professor shouted. He took off toward the monster.

But as the Professor flew in, the monster turned and shot him with his fire breath.

"Watch out!" the Girls cried.

But the Professor's white suit had fire-shielding. The flames didn't hurt him at all.

"Go get him, Professor!" Buttercup called.

The Professor zoomed around the monster. Then the Girls got another surprise. The Professor shot laser beams out of his silver goggles, aiming them right at the monster! He cried out in pain.

"Woo-hoo!" the Girls shouted.

"Let's help the Professor finish him off!" Blossom called to her sisters. "Bubbles, sonic scream!"

Bubbles let out a scream that made the monster shrink in pain.

"Buttercup, hit him with a freeze-beam!" Blossom said.

Buttercup sent out an icy green beam from her hands. The monster froze in place.

"Professor, get him with . . . with . . . er, with whatever it is you've got," Blossom directed.

The Professor flew in and superkicked the monster in the head.

Blossom finished the job herself with a one-two punch to the monster's chest.

It was too much. The monster couldn't fight back. He began to overload.

"Duck and cover!" Blossom shouted.

Boom! The monster exploded into a pile of green goo.

"Yay!" the people of Townsville shouted.

The Girls rushed over to the Professor.

"What's going on?" Buttercup demanded.

"How did you do all that?" Blossom wanted to know.

"Where did you get that suit?" Bubbles asked.

"Now, Girls, calm down and let me tell you," the Professor replied, brushing the dust off his white suit. "You see, I've really missed getting to spend time with the three of you. So when you left the movie today, I had a terrific idea. If I can't beat 'em, I'll join 'em. So I went home and made this supersuit."

"So you have superstrength?" Buttercup asked.

"You bet," the Professor replied.

"And laser beams?" Blossom added.

"Uh-huh." The Professor nodded.

"And you can fly?" Bubbles asked excitedly.

"Yep. This outfit makes me just as strong and tough as any of my three Powerpuff Girls. So from now on, we'll get to spend lots of time together," the Professor told them. He gave the Girls a big hug.

"Yay!" the Girls yelled.

Great thinking, Professor. The family that fights crime together stays together!

Chapter 6

The next week was the best week ever for the Girls and the Professor. Whenever the Powerpuff hot line rang, all four of them were on the scene as a superpowered team! With the help of his white supersuit, the Powerpuff Professor was a great fighter. He flew at top speed. He delivered superstrong punches and kicks. His silver goggles gave him X-ray vision and superpowered laser beams.

Together they were battling monsters and capturing robbers. The Professor was unstoppable! The city loved him. And so did the Girls. Everything was working out great. Blossom, Bubbles, and Buttercup got to spend more time with their beloved Professor. And the Professor got to spend more time with his favorite girls.

One afternoon, as the Girls were enjoying a day off at home, the Powerpuff hot line went off. Blossom hurried to the phone.

"Blossom!" the Mayor shouted from the other end of the line. "You Girls and the Professor have to hurry. Mojo Jojo is on the loose!"

Mojo Jojo was a genius monkey supervillain. The town was always in trouble when he was around.

"We'll be right there, Mayor," Blossom promised.

The Professor burst into the room. He was wearing his supersuit, and he looked ready for action. "What's the latest, Girls?" he asked.

"Mojo's causing trouble," Blossom responded. "We'd better hurry."

In a flash, the four of them were off.

The three Powerpuff Girls and the Powerpuff Professor against Mojo! He doesn't stand a chance!

Downtown, Mojo was inside his hoversuit, blasting up Townsville with his laser gun. The suit was a special Mojo invention. It covered him head to toe and was made of superstrong material. There was a propeller on the top to keep Mojo hovering.

The people of Townsville were running in fear. Buildings were going up in flames.

"Ha-ha-ha, citizens of Townsville. You think you can get away from me! Well, you are wrong! You cannot get away!" Mojo cackled.

The townspeople tried to hide anywhere they could. Then suddenly, there was a familiar swooshing sound from above. Pink, blue, green, and white streaks crisscrossed the sky.

"Yay!" the crowd yelled. Townsville's favorite foursome was on the way.

"Buttercup, get ready to give Mojo a rock-'em-sock-'em power drive. Bubbles, you and I will do the Boomerang Buster. And Professor, you hit him with the Laser Lightshow," Blossom called out.

Buttercup flew up to Mojo in his hoversuit. She began to throw punches with all her superstrength. Mojo began to rock back and forth.

"Stop that punching at once!" Mojo screamed from inside the suit. "You are making me dizzy, and I have a low tolerance for motion sickness! Stop! Stop!" He shot at Buttercup with his laser gun, knocking her to the ground.

"That will teach you, pesky Girl! Bwa-ha-ha!" Mojo laughed.

But Mojo didn't laugh long. The Powerpuff Professor began shooting lasers from his goggles. He shot them in every direction, all over the city. The bouncing lights dazed Mojo. He was confused. He didn't know what to do.

With Mojo's guard down, Blossom and Bubbles continued with their part of the plan. Blossom picked up Bubbles and hurled her through the air at top speed, away from Mojo. Suddenly, Bubbles boomeranged, flying toward Mojo faster than ever.

Mojo saw Bubbles speeding toward him. His eyes grew big. Bubbles was going way too quickly. And she was headed straight for him. He had to get out of there — fast!

But nothing was working. Bubbles was closing in. "Oh, no!" Mojo squeaked. He shut his eyes and braced himself for impact.

BOOM!

"Curse you, Powerpuff Girls!" Mojo yelled as he tumbled toward the ground. His hoversuit smashed into a million pieces.

"Powerpuff Girls, you always foil my plans!" Mojo screamed. He stomped his

feet. "I'll get you, Powerpuff Girls! I will! I will!"

The Girls just smiled. They knew they had won again.

But suddenly, the Professor spoke up. "You stop being mean to my little Girls, Mojo! Otherwise I'll get you!"

The Girls were shocked.

What are you doing, Professor?

"Oh, really?" Mojo said, laughing. "So now the Powerpuff Girls have their daddy to protect them? How sweet."

"That's right, Mojo," the Professor said. "Anybody who hurts my Girls will have to answer to me!"

"What's he doing?" Bubbles whispered.

"I don't know," Blossom replied, stunned.

"He's making us look like a bunch of babies!" Buttercup complained.

"Well, Powerpuff Girls, I guess I'll come back to fight you when you're all grown up. Maybe then your daddy will let you act like big girls. Bwa-ha-ha!" Mojo cackled as the police led him away.

The Girls were *so* embarrassed. Why had the Professor said that? They were superheroes, not babies.

Buttercup opened her mouth to say something to the Professor.

But Blossom put her hand on her sister's arm, stopping her.

"Well, I sure told Mojo," the Professor said proudly. He flew off, smiling.

But the Girls weren't smiling.

chapter 7

Later that evening, Blossom, Buttercup, and Bubbles were getting ready for bed.

"I can't believe the Professor said all that embarrassing stuff about us," Buttercup complained. She scowled.

"It wasn't very nice of him to treat us like babies," Bubbles agreed. She hugged her stuffed octopus.

"Let's just forget about it," Blossom told her sisters. "I'm sure he won't do it again."

41

But the next day, the Professor *did* do it again.

They had just finished catching some robbers who were trying to hold up the Townsville Bank. The Professor walked over to the robbers and began shaking his finger. "You guys better watch out. These Girls are my sweet little angels. If you ever hurt them again, you'll be in big trouble."

They may be angels, Professor, but they're also the Powerpuff Girls.

The robbers burst out laughing. "Poor little Powerpuffs. Now you need your daddy to protect you?" They kept laughing as the police dragged them away.

"Don't say anything to him," Blossom insisted to her sisters. "I'm sure he'll stop."

But things only got worse the next day, when the Girls and the Professor were in the middle of fighting a terrible three-headed monster.

"Bubbles, do your sonic scream," Blossom directed. "Buttercup, get him with a green beam. And Professor — "

But before she could finish, the Professor interrupted. "No, no, Blossom. You Girls go sit down. I don't want you getting any scrapes or bruises. I'll go fight the mean monster."

"What?" Buttercup yelled in astonishment.

"That's right," the Professor said. "I don't want my little Girls getting hurt."

"But — " Buttercup started to say.

But this time Blossom interrupted her. "Okay, Professor," Blossom agreed.

The Girls sat on the side as the Professor battled the three-headed monster.

"I can't believe this!" Buttercup fumed.

"This is awful!" Even Bubbles was mad.

"It's just a phase he's going through," Blossom assured them. "He'll probably get over it."

It soon became clear that the Professor couldn't defeat the three-headed monster on his own. Blossom, Bubbles, and Buttercup happily sprang into action.

Blossom flew by the monster's heads, delivering a swift kick to each head.

"Good kicks there, monkey-doodle!" the Professor shouted to her.

Blossom looked shocked.

"Monkey-doodle? That's a good one. Go get 'em, monkey-doodle!" Buttercup teased.

Blossom scowled at her sister.

Bubbles hit the monster with a super-powered ray beam.

"Great work, booger-bear!" the Professor yelled out to her.

"Booger-bear! Ha! That one's even better!" Buttercup cackled with delight.

Bubbles glared at Buttercup.

Then the monster came after Butter-cup. She turned and gave him a fierce punch in the eye.

"Wow!" the Professor shouted. "That was a super punch

45

there, lumpy-pie!"

"Lumpy-pie!" Bubbles and Blossom were laughing like crazy.

Lumpy-pie!

"Lumpy-pie! Lumpy-pie!" the crowd below chanted, taking up the nickname.

"Lumpy-pie! Lumpy-pie!" the monster taunted.

Buttercup was furious.

"Calm down, Buttercup," Blossom advised. "He's just rooting for us."

"With those stupid baby names?" Buttercup said.

"Well, at least he's letting us fight," Bubbles pointed out.

Buttercup was angry. But her sisters

had a point. At least the Professor wasn't making them sit on the sidelines anymore.

"Think of it this way," Blossom said. "It can't get any worse, right?"

Oh, but it could.

"Come on, let's go get him, my little cutie-cakes!" the Professor shouted.

"Go, cutie-cakes, go!" the crowd shouted.

The Girls were furious. But what could they do? They had to keep fighting.

So Blossom, Buttercup, and Bubbles fought faster and better than ever. At long last, they defeated the monster.

On the way home, the Professor gushed about

their great work. "You three were wonderful! You're the best little superheroes
ever!"

The Professor went on and on. But the
Girls didn't hear a word he said. They
were only thinking about one thing. The
Professor had to be stopped. Something
had to be done.

But what?

chapter 8

The next day, at Pokey Oaks Kindergarten . . .

Blossom called Buttercup and Bubbles together for a Powerpuff powwow.

"Girls, I think it's clear we have a problem," she began.

"A problem! That's putting it lightly!" Buttercup cried. "The Professor is making a mess of everything. First he won't let us fight. Then he starts calling us those sugary-sweet names in front of everyone. It's awful!"

49

"Well, I kinda like being called sweety-weety," Bubbles said. "But only when I'm being tucked in at night."

"So we all agree," Blossom said. "The question is, how do we tell him we don't need him without hurting his feelings?"

"We could send him a gift basket," Bubbles suggested.

"No, Bubbles. The Professor is a grown-up. I say we tell it to him straight," Buttercup said.

"We can't just come right out and tell him," Blossom said. "But maybe we can show him. I think I have the perfect plan."

The following day!
Beep! Beep! Beep!
The Powerpuff hot line went off. But before any of the Girls could reach the

phone, the Professor had picked it up.

"The super-duper Powerpuff hot line!" he answered eagerly. "Home of the best little superheroes in the world!"

The Girls rolled their eyes.

"Professor!" the Mayor yelled from the other end of the line. "Mojo Jojo is on the loose again. Hurry!"

"All right, Mayor, be right there," the Professor replied. "Girls, it's Mojo Jojo. I don't know if I want you three fighting that mean monkey again. He's dangerous."

"Gee, Professor, if we promise to be careful, can we come along?" Blossom asked.

"Well, okay," the Professor said. "But you Girls stay to the side. I don't want you getting hurt." He flew off.

Buttercup scowled. "This had better work, Blossom," she said as the girls took off after the Professor.

Downtown, Mojo was tearing up the town in his Robo Jojo, a giant destructor robot he had built.

"Not so fast, Mojo Jojo!" Blossom yelled as the Girls flew in to attack.

"Bwaaa-haaa-haaa-haaa! Powerpuff Girls, you thought you had defeated me. But I am not defeated. I am still here! It is you who will be defeated!"

The Powerpuff Professor cut in.

"Mojo!" the Professor called out. "You come here and fight me! I don't want you hurting my sweet little pumpkins!"

"Sorry, Professor, but I've got the perfect recipe for Powerpuff pumpkin pie!" Mojo said. "I've just got to try it out." He shot a giant ray from his Robo Jojo. It knocked all three Girls to the ground.

The Girls lay there motionless.

Girls! Get up! What about your plan? What are you going to do now?

"Powerpuff Girls, I have finally gotten you!" Mojo yelled. "You thought it was you who had gotten me. But you were wrong. Now there is nothing to stop me from taking over the world!"

"Not so fast, Mojo Jojo!" the Professor said, heading toward the Robo Jojo.

"Oh, yes, the Powerpuff Professor. I must defeat you before I complete my plan," Mojo laughed. "But this should be as easy as squishing your little pumpkins!"

The Professor wasn't going to let Mojo

get away with hurting his Girls. "You just hold onto your helmet, Mojo, and be prepared for a fight!" he yelled.

"Okay, Professor, let's see what you've got," Mojo replied. He shot a ray from his Robo Jojo.

The ray hit the Professor hard. He was thrown back and smashed into a building. When he opened his eyes, he saw Mojo coming after him in the giant robot.

"Ha-ha, Professor," Mojo cackled. "You're not all that tough, are you?"

"Easy thing to say from inside a robot," the Professor said, rubbing his aching shoulders. He was down, but not out. "Why don't you come out and fight me, monkey against man?"

Mojo looked offended. "What? Do you think I need this machine to beat you? Well, you are wrong. I am Mojo Jojo! I can beat you, Powerpuff Professor. Just you wait and see!" Mojo climbed out of his robot, ready to fight.

The two of them went at it. Mojo was much stronger than the Professor had ever imagined. He had great strength and fast moves. He punched and kicked better than any monkey in the world. The Professor was taking quite a beating. His silver suit was designed to withstand powerful forces like laser beams from far away. But a one-on-one boxing match was a different story.

Meanwhile, the Powerpuff Girls still lay on the ground, motionless.

Or, wait a minute — is Bubbles peeking?

Mojo cackled a deep monkey laugh. "You see, Powerpuff Professor, you are not such a hotshot after all," he boasted. "In fact, here's a hotshot worth bragging about." He pulled out a tiny ray gun and shot at the Professor.

But the ray bounced off the Professor's suit. It hit Mojo, knocking him to the ground.

The Professor saw his advantage. With his last ounce of strength, he socked Mojo. The monkey slammed into buildings and streaked across the sky. It wasn't the best punch he'd ever thrown, but it was enough to send Mojo flying.

"So, you thought that was a hotshot, Mojo?" the Professor said wearily. "Try this one on for size."

As Mojo struggled to get to his feet, the Professor shot him with lasers from his silver goggles. Mojo collapsed, defeated.

Great job, Professor! But . . . are you okay?

The Professor flew over to where Blossom, Buttercup, and Bubbles lay.

"Are you all right, Girls?" the Professor asked anxiously.

Blossom's eyelids fluttered open. "Um, yes, I think so," she said.

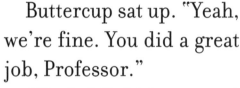

Buttercup sat up. "Yeah, we're fine. You did a great job, Professor."

"Yeah," Bubbles agreed with a big smile. "You really showed that Mojo."

"You really are a great superhero," Blossom added. "We can't wait to see what you do next time."

"Oh, well, thanks, Girls," the Professor replied. He rubbed his neck. "But I don't think there'll be any next time."

"What?" Blossom asked.

"You're quitting?" Buttercup said.

"But why?" Bubbles asked innocently.

"Fighting crime is really, really hard work," the Professor said. He groaned and rubbed his neck again. "I may be good, but I wasn't made for it like you Girls were. It really makes me tired. And my muscles get so sore!"

"But Professor — "

"No, no, Girls," the Professor said. "There are bills to pay, and the dishes are piling up. And the lab! I have to work on some experiments. Sorry, Girls, but I'm hanging up my supersuit for the last time."

As the Girls carried him home, the Professor rubbed his muscles and moaned. Being a superhero was so exhausting! He soon fell sound asleep.

The Girls exchanged glances.

"Well, it worked," Blossom whispered.

"The Powerpuff Professor is history," Buttercup agreed. "What a relief."

"Yeah," Bubbles said. "I am going to miss spending time with the Professor, though."

"Hey, let's ask him to take us to see the rest of *The TV Puppet Pals Movie* tomorrow," Blossom suggested.

"Cool," Buttercup agreed.

The Girls took off in a streak of pink, blue, and green. They were content to be a trio once more.

So once again the day is saved, thanks to the Powerpuff Girls!